THIS IGLOO BOOK BELONGS TO:

....

igloobooks

Written by Stephanie Moss
Illustrated by Claudia Ranucci

Designed by Hannah George
Edited by Hannah Campling

Copyright © 2018 Igloo Books Ltd

An imprint of Igloo Books Group,
part of Bonnier Books UK
bonnierbooks.co.uk

Published in 2019
by Igloo Books Ltd, Cottage Farm
Sywell, NN6 0BJ
Manufactured in China. GUA009 0519
10 9 8 7 6 5 4 3 2 1

Library of Congress Cataloging-in-Publication
Data is available upon request.

ISBN 978-1-83852-526-2
IglooBooks.com
bonnierbooks.co.uk

The BEST PARTY in the WORLD

igloobooks

Little Mouse was lonely and spent most days on her own.
She had a quiet life in her mouse hole, all alone.

Best Friends

One day, she wrote an invitation and inside it said,

"Come to my tea party tomorrow. See you soon!" she read.

She addressed it to her mouse friend
to send the letter on its way.

Then she gave it to the Mail Mouse
on his first stop of the day.

Before he delivered it, he stopped for a bite of cheese.

Then it flew . . .

Petal Cottage
2 Acorn Lane
Bluebell Woods
BFF M1CE

whoosh

. . . out of his bag on a sudden gust of breeze.

"Look!" they said to Rooster, who raised the party alarm.

Once the sheep and horses knew, it was all over the farm!

Then Sheepdog took the letter and ran over to the woods
to tell as many of his friends about the party as he could.

Fox passed the invite on to Deer, who showed Squirrel in her tree.
Owl woke up from her nap and said, "A party? **Yay! Yippee!**"

She flew over to the dock, where a ship was setting sail.
The letter journeyed through the waves, carried by a friendly whale.

He gave it to a seagull friend
just as she was passing by.

SQUAWK! she went excitedly
and flew into the sky.

She reached the sandy shore and dried the invite in the sun.

As soon as she showed the monkeys, they knew it would be fun!

Their jungle friends joined in and said, "A party sounds just great!
Maybe if we leave right now, we might not be too late."

By the next afternoon, the guests all started to appear.
They'd come from all around the world, each full of happy cheer.

"You must be here for the party!" one called, dancing in the queue.
"I can't wait," replied the next. "It will be so great. **Woo-hoo!**"

Meanwhile, their noisy voices caused the mouse hole walls to shake.

When Little Mouse opened her door
she knew there must be some mistake.

"What are you doing here?" she asked. She couldn't believe her eyes!
"I'm having a small tea party. This is quite a big surprise!"

"We got your invitation," they said. "We thought it was so kind!"
"Well my house is only small," she said. "I hope that you don't mind?"

They all **squashed** and **squished** to fit.

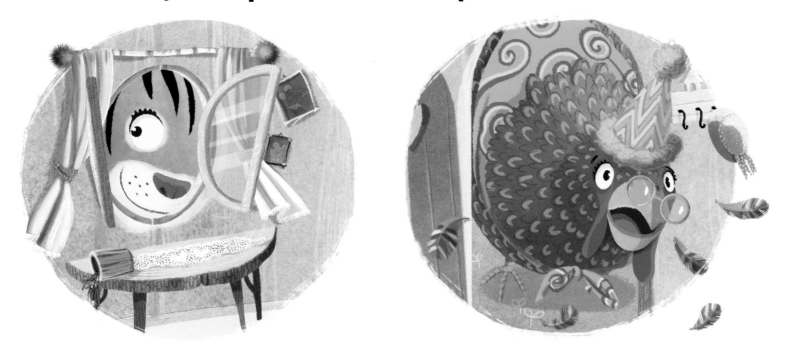

"There's no room!" the animals cried.

"There's only one thing to do," said Little Mouse. "Let's party outside!"

So Little Mouse and her new friends partied long into the night.
They laughed and sang and danced together, till the morning light.

It was the party of a lifetime, with guests both big and small.
And a mix-up in the mail was what had started it all.